FRANK CARTER: CHAPTER 4

YASHESH RATHOD

Made with ❤ on the Notion Press Platform
www.notionpress.com

I dedicate my work to my father, Dinesh Rathod, my mother, Pramila Rathod and my sister, Aesha Rathod

Contents

A Good News

I sat at a round table in the shop of Eliza, the fortune teller. She sat across the table in front of me, a crystal ball lying on a stand on the table in between us. I had just fought an epic battle with Sirius and his pet dragon with the help of the divine tigress, and I had managed to win it. I had decided that before going home I would see Eliza and return her amulet with the pellets of power. I was handing back the magical amulet to Eliza when she said something that would be good news for me to hear post the bloody battle with an ancient time deity.

'I know what you're grieving about deep in your heart. The loss of your friends named Randolph and Athena is giving you pain, isn't it?'

By now I knew she could read thoughts, so I nodded sadly.

'Today is your lucky day, dear, 'cause I'm gonna tell you something that you will like very much,' Eliza said.

'What's that?' I asked.

'There is a way to fetch souls of the deceased who haven't been dead for more than six months. All of the souls are collected by the soul collector and they stay there until he, the soul collector, makes use of the souls in the reincarnation process. Once reincarnation is complete, the souls enter into new bodies. Before a month from the day of the death, you could make a bargain with the soul collector for any soul if you brought to him a heart of a special monstrous creature called "Mrunna" for each soul,' Eliza said.

I stood up in excitement at the hope of seeing Randolph and Athena alive again. 'Tell me more,' I said excitedly.

'Sit down, dear, and I will tell you everything about it,' Eliza said while trying to calm me down.

I obeyed and sat down and began listening carefully to what Eliza would say next.

'The monster lives in another realm called Rethnia, the same realm where you will find the soul collector known as "Dar". Once presented with the hearts of Mrunnas, you will be given your friend's souls in a special earthen jar. Take that jar to the dead bodies and open it and the souls will enter the bodies,' Eliza explained.

'How do I get to this realm called Rethnia?' I asked.

With that question, Eliza stood up and rummaged through items on the shelves at the back wall of her shop. After a full minute, she returned to her chair at the table.

'This is how you will get to the Rethnia,' Eliza said while handing me a necklace with a pendant in the shape of lighting.

'What's this?'

'It's a talisman to enter other realms,' explained Eliza. 'You will see the inscription in greek on the pendant. It is a powerful chant to let you enter any realm. All it needs is the touch of a thing of the realm you wish to enter, and when a droplet of blood is fed to the pendent it glows and transforms you to the realm that thing belongs to,' she explained.

'If I've got it right, then, you're saying that I will be needing something belonging to the realm Rethnia?' I asked stupidly.

'Yes, dear' she said.

'How do I do it? I mean getting my hands on an object belonging to another realm?' I asked.

'Don't worry, dear. I happen to have objects belonging to over a hundred realms, including Rethnia too,' Eliza said smiling.

'How did you get them all?' I asked in surprise.

'I don't need any object from the realm to travel there. I do it with my mere mind. Decades of practice I have had for doing that, been collecting objects from the realms as trophies. This pendant is the creation of mine for those who don't know magic and still wish to enter another realm,' Eliza explained.

'Your magical craft reminds me of my friend Randolph Smith,' I said.

'He is not the only one with magical skills, you know,' she said smiling. Once again she stood up and tried to find something on the shelves at the back wall of her shop. Moments later she returned with a piece of rock in her hand. She handed it to me and said, 'You're good to go once you have spilt a droplet of blood on that pendant while keeping that piece of rock touched to it,' she explained.

'Hold on a second. You say a monster to slay, and how I'm going to do it?' I asked.

'Of course, you're going to need something powerful for that and that's why I'm going to give you my magical amulet for one more adventure of yours,' she said and stretched her left hand over the round table towards me, amulet resting in her palm.

I picked the amulet that had been offered to me by Eliza and tied the lace of it around my neck.

'Now you once again will have the powers of Aura of Shiv, Bow of Rama and the wings of Angels and using them you could kill the three Mrunnas and gain their hearts to offer them to the soul collector,' she said.

I nodded and took a blade from Eliza and made a small cut into my forearm to let a droplet of blood fall onto the lighting-shaped pendant. The pendant glowed brightly as soon as I made the rock contact with the pendant. The glow increased to the point that I was blinded by its white brightness. Next thing I knew my mind was travelling fast through a blue tube made of greek letters surrounded by white light. It went on for quite some time and I could do nothing but see the nauseating view of me passing through a tube. When it was over I was again blinded by bright white light and when I opened my eyes I found myself in the heart of a jungle. I tied the pendant's lace around my neck and hid the small rock inside my pants pocket.

No sooner had I taken a few steps than a booby trap hidden beneath the leafy ground triggered and I was lifted and hung upside down five meters from the ground.

'Billy, the trap has triggered,' came the shout. Moments later, from my upside-down view, I saw two men striding toward me in excitement. But as soon as they saw me swinging by the rope, their excitement turned into frustration.

'This is the seventh time in a week the trap caught the wrong target, Billy,' the first man said while shaking his head in disbelief.

In response to the man's comment the other man, who must be Billy, slapped his forehead with his own palm, showing frustration. 'Common, man, this can't be happening. I've not eaten for days and if I don't get a dear, rabbit or something today, I might die of starvation, Jimmy.'

The first man who must be Jimmy said while placing his hands on his stomach, 'I'm hungry too, brother, So hungry that I would eat a whole sea whale.'

Both men were so busy discussing the hunger problems that they completely had forgotten that I hung painfully upside down. 'Guys, a little help here?' I requested.

'Oh right! Jimmy, cut the lad down with your new fancy knife, will ya?' Billy said.

Jimmy climbed up the tree trunk while holding an exquisite-looking small knife between his teeth and cut me down. Billy had set a bundle of soft grass beneath me on the ground to absorb my fall.

When I had dusted off my clothes, Billy asked me, 'Who are you and what the lad of your age doing here in the middle of this jungle?'

I thought for a few seconds before coming up with an answer, 'I've come from across the sea and my name is Frank.'

'What made you travel across the sea to be here?' Billy asked.

'I'm looking for creatures called Mrunnas,' I decided to tell the truth.

'For what?' asked Jimmy.

'I wish to slay a couple of Mrunas,' I said.

'Let me guess. You wish to present their hearts to Dar, the soul collector, in order to bring somebody back from the dead?' Billy asked.

'How do you know?' I asked.

'You see, Mrunnas are found only in this kingdom, Kotwal ruled by king John. Every year, people and adventurers come here from far villages to slay these special creatures in order to bring their loved ones from the dead state. So, it is normal to have outsiders in our kingdom looking for Mrunnas,' explained Jimmy.

'But slaying those special creatures is forbidden here unless you are granted by the king himself to do so,' Billy explained.

'Why is it so?' I asked.

'Because they are of a rare and endangered species and Dar, the soul collector accepts only their hearts in exchange for the souls of dead ones. On the order of the king, those few numbered creatures are being saved for bringing someone important back to life,' Jimmy explained.

'But you could earn the chance of slaying them. You could enrol yourself for the arena competition where you fight other warriors pursuing the same thing as you are. Once you've defeated them all, you could enter a final trial of your choosing with various difficulties depending upon the number of Mrunnas you desire to slay,' Billy explained.

'But only fools would dare to enter the arena,' Jimmy said.

'Why is it so?' I asked.

'Because the competitions in the arena are to the death. Meaning that the loser not only loses the chance to kill Mrunna but also his life,' Jimmy explained.

I was shocked by hearing that. 'What if I tried to hunt one of the Mrunnas without the king's permission?

'Don't be daft. Don't even talk about such a thing in public,' Jimmy explained.

'You will become an outlaw, man! King will continue to send his men after you until you're caught and put behind bars in the prison in his dungeon. You even might get the death penalty after serving your sentence,' Billy explained grimly.

'My brother is right. It doesn't matter if it is a child or an old one, all of those who kill Mrunnas against the king's will will get punished badly,' Jimmy said.

There sounded a rumble of the stomach from Billy and he placed his hands over his belly, suggesting that he was starving.

'Look, I'm new here and don't know much about the surroundings. Would you take me to the arena so that I could enter the competition?' I requested.

There was silence immediately. Over the rustling of leaves created by the cool breeze, both brothers looked at each other for a moment before returning their gaze to me. 'Are you sure, lad? Are you sure you wanna do that?' Billy asked seriously.

After a moment of hesitation, I nodded.

'Okay, our house is no farther from the Arena. We might as well drop you at the arena's door,' Billy said.

'But first, help us to get a rabbit. You know they say "Save a man's appetite, save a man's soul". You help save ours and we help you. How does that sound?' Jimmy asked.

'Okay, that's fine with me,' I said and we three began hunting for a rabbit.

*

The rabbit was slowly being cooked by Jimmy over the campfire. It was night and both brothers were drolling with saliva with the prospect of having dinner after many days. I wasn't hungry, and I couldn't eat rabbits even if I were because I was a vegetarian.

The two brothers ate the cooked rabbit and satisfied their hunger. Afterwards, we talked to each other in front of the fire until the three of us drifted to sleep on the bare ground. Tomorrow, I shall enter my name into the contest at the arena and with the help of the magical amulet and the powers it wields, I would be able to defeat all of the contestants. But one thing worried me and it is the killing of other combatants I would have to perform to defeat them.

CHAPTER TWO

The Enrolment

I opened my eyes and was greeted by the warm light of the morning sun. Both brothers were packing up things in a big canvas bag. I stretched my limbs to get rid of remnants of sleep and stood up.

'Good morning, mate. Time to go,' Jimmy said.

I offered the two brothers my hand to pack things up and in a few minutes, we were on our way to the village.

It had been two hours of walking before I saw the first of the houses in the village. Their chimneys were emitting grey smoke. The whole scene reminded me of my village in my realm. At far and seemed to be in the middle of the village lay a giant circular building with no roof.

'Our house is just behind the arena,' Billy said while pointing at the large building, the top of which was shrouded with clouds.

'The architecture of the arena is that of an amphitheatre, but other than that there is nothing in common between the two of them. While in an amphitheatre, epics are rehearsed and played, there in the arena, deadly battles take place. While in an amphitheatre there is music and drama while in the arena there is death and blood. I would say the amphitheatre and the arena are like two siblings with quite opposite natures,' Jimmy explained.

'Who had it made, I mean the structure of that size?' I asked curiously the two brothers hoping that one of them would reply.

'It was made five centuries ago, by king Arun for the purpose of various sporting events but, ever since it was found that Mrunnas hearts' could be used to make dead people alive, it was later turned into a deadly arena for the game of winning rights at slaying Mrunnas,' Billy explained.

'There once were fifty thousand Mrunnas inhabited here in our kingdom's special guarded forest called Mrunnavan, but even the arena couldn't stop that number from falling to a mere five hundred. Ever since that fall in the Mrunnas' number, the arena's rule and the trials afterwards have become godly difficult,' Jimmy explained.

'Yeah, my brother is right. I haven't seen a man or woman getting past the trial post the arena victory in a decade. The greatest warriors have failed those unforgiving trials and I don't see how you're gonna make it past them,' Billy said.

'Heck, I don't even see you getting past your first fight in the arena,' Jimmy said.

'Don't worry, guys. I have some help,' I said smiling.

'What kind of help? No mate, nobody's allowed to help you while you're fighting in a contest to death,' Billy explained.

'No one is coming to help, it's just that I have a little magic on my side,' I said.

'Oh, so you're one of those mages. Never saw a mage this young though,' Jimmy said.

'There will be likes of you in the list of combatants there in the arena. The mages with more age and magic than yours at their disposal will be your toughest matches,' Billy said.

'Well, I just need to win the arena and get past the trials, and I want to get over the slaying of a couple of mrunnas as early as possible,' I said.

'There is no need for haste, mate. The last season finished just yesterday. And it will be quite some time before the next season will begin. The combatants around the world will come and register their names in the contest and there will be contracts signing and all, you know,' Billy said.

'And not to mention all the dried blood on the arena's battleground that the workers there will have absolute horror cleaning up before the next season starts,' Jimmy said.

'Oh... The blood of those combatants they must have seen while fighting,' Billy said shaking his head. 'How long until the next season starts, brother?'

'Approximately, after twenty to thirty days,' Jimmy replied.

'Who won that past season?' I asked curiously.

'A woman named Lilith. But she failed one of the three trials. However the trial doesn't kill ya, and she got to keep her life. Chances are high that she will be trying again in the next season. If you come face to face with her in the arena, then you might as well forfeit and keep your life because she is an expert in throwing knives and her martial skills are way up there with the gods,' Jimmy replied.

'I'll keep that in mind,' I said while nodding. She reminded me of Athena who was equally talented with knives and martial skills.

When we reached the double door of the arena, there was a long queue of people. 'They are the agents of the contestants enrolling their clients' names into the contest. We will be waiting for you while you stand in line. We will be waiting near the door by the clerk who is enrolling the names and when it's your number in the line, we will take over. Just think about the battles you're gonna have, and leave the managing and talking to us,' Billy said.

'Why would you help me? I'm a complete stranger to you, after all,' I said.

'At the end of each fight you've fought and won, you will have gained fight money from the bets that are put on the battle by the spectators. We want half of what you will gain. What do you say? Deal?' Jimmy said.

My goal wasn't the money here after all, so I nodded my agreement to that.

'Now, we're talking. Okay, stand in line now. You better start working out and what better way to do that than start with your legs by standing in a long line?' Billy said.

I stood in the line and waited as the line moved worse than the speed of a snail. Once in a while, there were shouts from the angry people ahead telling the clerk sitting at a wooden table to hurry up the process of enrollment.

Finally, after a time that seemed like an aeon, my number came up, and Billy and Jimmy wasted no time and started talking.

'This lad is our client and we wish to enrol him into the contest of arena,' Billy said bluntly.

The clerk rested his back on the chair and with both hands rested on his head, gave out a cruel laughter. 'A lad doesn't belong in here. This is the palace for big boys and girls, no offence,' came the reply from the clerk, his eyes staring at me insultingly.

'No, you don't understand, Rafiq. This lad is capable of battle here in the arena,' Billy said.

'Yes, my brother is right. The lad's got magic. He's a mage of a high level,' said Jimmy.

'If that's so then you wouldn't mind demonstrating the small amount of your skill, would ya?' Rafiq, the clerk, said.

'Of course, he is gonna show you some, aren't you, mighty...Frank...the mage...from ...across the sea?' Billy said while struggling to grope for the words to make him sound a little heroic.

I did as they told and let out a shot from the bow of Rama up in the air. After a few moments, the arrow hurled from my invisible bow blasted into the clouds with the sound of distant thunder.

The two brothers were still staring up, trying to figure out what had just happened, while the clerk began processing to enrol my name into the arena quickly after the showcase of my magical powers.

Finally, a royal stamp was made onto the paper and given to me. 'Take good care of that paper,' Rafiq said. 'If you lose it, you lose your chance to battle in the arena.'

'Yes, sir,' I nodded.

'I will be seeing you right back here with other contestants after twenty days and twenty nights when the next season opens up and these arena doors have been swung open. Until then, get yourself a nice place to live and keep practising your combat skills. I'm off to arena's office quarters now,' the clerk said, stood up from his wooden chair, picked up a pile of registration papers, balancing them with the help of his chest, and left awkwardly.

When Rafiq had entered the arena from another small single door far, Both brothers turned to me. 'Any idea where you're gonna spend these twenty days and nights?' Jimmy asked.

'I know a couple of good lodging not far from here. They are cheap, moneywise, not by way of the quality of service they provide,' Billy suggested.

I had forgotten to pack any money with me. I had not thought that I would need any. 'I've got no money,' I said and hung my head. A moment later I felt a light pat on my back and heard Billy's voice say, 'Don't sweat about it, mate. You could stay with us at our house. But you've gotta earn your keep by doing some chores in the house and helping us with the fishing,' Jimmy said.

My mood cheered up at that offer. 'Of course, I could help you out with those. Thanks, guys.' I said.

'Then it's a deal!' Billy said.

'Right, this way, please,' Jimmy said and led the way to their house.

We passed a maze-like mesh of streets flanked by houses of all shapes and sizes before we arrived at the front door of a small cottage.

'Welcome to our home,' Billy said. 'It's not much but at least you will have a roof over your head until the arena season starts. It's not as bad inside as it looks from the outside. I hope you will like it,' Billy said.

With a key turned in the lock, the door was opened. it was a little gloomy inside. There was only one window in the far wall but it had been closed, must be to prevent anything or anyone from breaking into the cottage.

'Jimmy, open up that window to get some sunlight and fresh air going inside the house,' Billy ordered. 'Meanwhile, I will go ahead and fill up the lanterns with kerosene for the evening.'

I just stood there while both men busied themselves with the chores. 'May I offer you a hand?' I asked.

'Sure, mate. Grab that broom and give a good sweep across the floor. We haven't been home for a few days and the place might have collected plenty of dust,' Billy said.

'And watch out for mice. Those little fiends somehow always manage to break into the house no matter how much air-packed we seal the cottage,' Jimmy said.

'Just once I would like to know their secret passage from where they are entering here,' Billy shook his ball of fist threateningly in the air while his eyes scanned the floor for any mouse.

After I had picked the broom up from a corner, we all three got really busy for an hour or so before everything was clean, tidy and in its place inside the cottage. Jimmy had thumped into the wall while trying to catch a mouse.

Having to do nothing, we all dozed off during the afternoon in the cottage and decided to get out for fishing just an hour prior to the sunset at the nearby lake called Kaveri.

In a bag of black cloth, we had all the fish traps, nets and all the things we needed to catch some fish. With the bag slung over behind my back, I followed the two twin brothers who led me through the beautiful village of theirs and to Kaveri.

When we reached the lake, I was astonished by its beauty. The water reflected the golden light of the soon-to-be setting sun. The place was crowded with fishermen and we had a hard time finding a spot for ourselves. But when we found the spot, we settled and once ready, threw the fishing net into the lake and waited silently.

As the partial orange and partial yellow sun sank slowly towards the horizon, one by one fishermen started to pack up and leave. We were the last ones to pack up with no luck with fish.

'Hurry up, mate. We are late. Oh, we are late,' Billy said hysterically while packing things up.

'What is he worried about? It's just evening,' I asked Jimmy.

'It's not about that. It's about the Rak,' Jimmy replied. 'My brother has every right to be worried at this time.'

'Rak? What's that?' I asked.

'Our village is haunted by this monster kind called Rak after the sun sets,' Jimmy said.

'Raks are bad news. Really bad news. They get you once they get their eyes on you and start chewing at your flesh like huge rats. And the thing is you're still alive when they start to eat you,' Billy said while shaking with fear.

'Only thing that can save you is the sunlight or the light from the lantern, torch or candle. Lights burn up their skins so they keep their distance from them,' Jimmy said.

'But once you're out of light...' Billy made a cross sign with his hand. 'God, help you,' Billy continued grimly.

'Enough talk and get a lantern lit, Billy,' Jimmy ordered. And no sooner he had said that than in the darkness across the lake came a bone-chilling roar of something which I figured to be of one of the Raks.

With shaky hands, Billy lit up the lantern and then guided by the radius of the latent light, we silently made our way back to the cottage.

CHAPTER THREE

Raks

It was when we had entered the cottage that the two brothers' hysteria relaxed. Two lanterns were lit afterwards inside the cottage after locking the front door. The grilled window lay open to make a room for fresh air and keep us from being suffocated. It was a long evening and night and we had nothing to do but get into bed early. Before I got into bed I had peered out from the open grilled window and saw that the whole street was empty. Everyone was inside his or her house. No one was seen venturing outside. The windows of all the houses illuminated with bright light, suggesting that they feared the raks as much as the twin brothers did, and to keep those demons away they had lit lanterns and candles and left them lit over the night.

Outside the terrifying roars of raks would continue to sound here and there until the morning. Once or twice the roars were so loud that we thought the rak was right outside the front door or behind the grilled window. None of us had dared to lift the shawl we were sleeping under to check.

Even I was so terrified that the whole night I had stayed awake with my eyelids closed. We only opened our eyes and lifted the shawl when there were roosters started crowing which suggested the morning.

'Had a good night's sleep, mate?' Jimmy asked me.

'Not really. Those demonic roars kept waking me up from time to time over the night,' I replied.

'Same here,' Billy admitted.

'Look, we're going for a bath at lake Kaveri. Wanna join us in washing the filth of the body?' Jimmy asked.

I may tolerate many things but one thing I could not that was being dirty. I always liked to keep clean so I nodded.

'Very well, then. Grab those clothes of mine from the cupboard. I think they will fit ya. You're gonna need fresh clothes after the bath. Putting on dirty clothes after a bath has no meaning of having cleansed your body. So go ahead take 'em,' Jimmy said.

I did as he had said and took a shirt and a pair of trousers and after picking up the necessary things for the bath we left.

Upon reaching the lake, there were a couple of guys already swimming in the water. As I was watching them, the two brothers took the clothes off and with a splash dived into the lake. Jimmy called me to join him in the water, so I took my clothes but left my inner clothes on and jumped in.

It had been for fifteen minutes we had enjoyed the lake before we dressed up in the fresh clothes we had brought along. I had left my belongings, that is the earthen soul jar and the pendant, which I would need to return to my realm, inside a trunk Billy had given me at the cottage. But I still wore the amulet of power.

'Feels fresh after the bath, isn't it?' Jimmy asked.

I nodded but a part of my mind was thinking about the terror of raks. How these demons terrorised the everyday life of this village. I vowed to sort it out once and for all. So my next question was, 'Is there a way to get rid of these raks?'

'If you're brave enough to go near their nest in the mountains,' Billy said.

'Yeah, there probably hundreds of them there resting during the daylight inside the gloom of the caves of the mountain,' Jimmy explained.

'How far are these caves from here?' I asked.

'It's at the edge of the village up north. Why. You can't be with your sane mind thinking about taking out a horde of them, are you?' Jimmy asked.

'I do,' I replied bravely.

'It's madness, my friend, madness I tell ya,' Billy said.

'My brother is right. Don't be daft. These raks have terrorized the village for centuries. Many have tried this foolish attempt you're suggesting to put up a fight against them but none have succeeded. They are just too demonic and powerful,' Jimmy said.

'To know that you just need to see one, and the sense will get knocked into you telling you that it's madness to even think of such an outlandish thing of putting up a fight against them,' Billy said and began heading towards the cottage.

*

We were safely tucked into the cottage once it was sunset and the light began to fail. I had just had some vegetables brought up by Jimmy while Billy cooked them for me. The two brothers ate a fish each that they had caught in the afternoon at Kaveri while I tucked in my vegetables. The streets began to become deserted one by one and I heard people bar the doors of the houses one after another. After half an hour it was like midnight outside. Not a bird was seen outside.

Soon, the hellish roars began suggesting that the raks had entered the village. But my attention was caught by a scream of a boy. 'What's that?' I asked immediately.

'Must be a poor small boy, who must have failed to return to his home in time,' Billy said while the scream of the small boy continued.

'Isn't anybody gonna help to save him?' I asked, anger rising in my body like bile at the inability to do anything by anybody.

'No, brother, he's long gone. A rak has caught him. Nothing can be done now about it,' Jimmy said while shaking his head.

I heard the parents yelling frantically behind the windows of their home at the helpless child, 'Somebody, save him. Save my child. Save... save Jeremy.'

I couldn't stand by and watch the scene being played before me, so I asked the two brothers to unlock the door. The two brothers tried to talk me down out of this but when they saw anger boiling in my eyes and the determination in my voice, they obeyed and let me out. No sooner had I stepped over the threshold than the door was shut by the two brothers behind my back.

I unfurled my wings of angels and took flight. Without wasting any time, I flew right in the direction of the boy's scream. In the air, I finally spotted a rak who's got the boy. They were like huge-sized bats. The boy was held into the clutches of the talons and was being carried towards the distant mountains.

The caves, I said to myself. It must be taking the poor boy to the caves in the mountains the twin brothers have talked about. With that thought, I darted like an arrow towards the target and within a moment I was above the rak. But when I thought of attacking the rak with the bow of Rama, another rak attacked me first. An aerial fight took place. The rak sought to destroy my face with its razor-sharp talons. But the Aura of Shiv helped me by building a shield around my body. When we separated I quickly put some distance between me and the rack and charged a shot from the bow of Rama and let go. With a bright light and Kaboom, the rak exploded into pieces.

Next, more of them attack me. The aura of the shield could take only so much, so I retreated and tried to shake them off my trail. Once again I continued to charge shot after shot from the bow of Rama, taking out up to two raks at a time.

After some struggle from the both sides, the surviving raks left the fight and headed back to the caves in the mountains. While keeping my distance I followed them.

Upon reaching one of the caves, I decided to enter it. The moonlight shone on the inside of the cave with its silver light. I had to save that kid, I said to myself. So, slowly with a tip-toed style of a cat, I walked into the cave and began searching it thoroughly.

When I came across the body of the boy, I was too late. Its head was the only thing left, and the whole body had been chewed up to the bones. Three of the raks were still feeding off the boy's dead body. I couldn't help myself but gasp loudly and the attention of those three raks turned to me. Their fiery red eyes glowed brightly in the darkness. I lost my courage when I saw behind the three a legion. A legion of raks was hung from the cave's ceiling. There must have been thousands of them inside of just one cave. I just ran deliriously to get to the safety of the twin brothers' cottage. While running, one of them from behind managed to scratch my back with their sharp talons, and I had to bite my lip to let out a cry of pain.

I barely made it alive. It was stupid of me to go into their hive like that. I could've been ripped into pieces if it hadn't been for the powers from the amulet. I flew into the sky and made my way back to the cottage. From the sky, I saw the whole village empty. Not a single animal like a dog or a cat could be seen.

When I reached the door, I thumped loudly once and all of a sudden feinted to the ground outside the door.

*

When I opened my eyes, I observed that I was lying in a bed, being nursed by Jimmy. I asked what had happened.

'You were poisoned right at the moment you got attacked by the venomous tallon from one of the raks,' Jimmy said.

Billy entered the cottage. 'Hey, you've come to. Good. The doctor has been saying you would awake by today,' Billy said.

'How long I have been out?' I asked while sitting up.

'Three days,' Billy said. 'I arranged a doctor the other day and he has been checking on you since then. You almost terrified us when you dropped dead like that.'

'Yeah. I told you it was a bad idea going after that rak,' Jimmy said.

'What happened? Did you find the boy?' Billy asked.

'He ... didn't make it,' I said hanging my head.

For a moment there was a silence, but then came the voice of Billy, 'You did something no one would ever do in their sanity. I am proud of you. And for the boy, there was nothing you could do more. You did your best but the kid had death written in his destiny.'

'That night I saw something,' I said.

'What?' both brothers asked together.

'I saw a legion of raks. Probably thousands of them. And that was only in a single cave. God knows how many such caves are there,' I said shuddering at the mere thought.

Billy had his jaw dropped to the floor while Jimmy put both his hands on the top of his head and rolled his eyes to the ceiling.

'I guess there is no way to destroy those dark flying demons, is there,' Billy said.

'Unless you gather an army of mrunnas to attack their nest,' Jimmy joked but no one found it funny.

In fact, I found it very genius. 'Say again?!' I asked him to repeat the sentence.

'Gather an army of mrunnas to attack their nest??' Jimmy repeated.

'Are mrunnas that powerful?' I asked.

'Half a dozen can easily take out the entire raks' nest. But why? You can't be seriously thinking of gathering a mrunnas' army, are you?' Billy asked.

'No one has thought of it because it is a ridiculous idea. A mrunna would thump you into the ground like a bolt if it saw you,' Jimmy said.

'No kidding, mate. They are like three-storeyed building tall white apes. Powerful enough to thump you with its hammer fist six feet deep into the ground. There you will have your funeral done right there,' Billy said.

'Good luck persuading them to your cause because they are as much animal as the dogs and cats are, and wouldn't understand a thing of man's language,' Jimmy said.

'Do they have their young with them?' I asked.

'Of course, they do. They may be animals but very socialized ones, but why?' Billy asked.

'You know my flying by now so, I'm planning to dress up like one of the raks and abduct one of the young ones. Then I will make them follow me all the way to the mountains, the raks' caves, during the night, when they will be out for the hunt.

'Coming face to face with each other, surely both kinds will attack each other for dominance. It will be one bloody battle, the one the raks will lose I hope,' I explained.

'But will the mrunnas fall for that?' Jimmy asked.

'They have to,' I said.

'But first, you're gonna need to win the arena battle to get anywhere near the mrunnas' sanctuary, unless once again I say this that if you wanna become an outlaw on this land,' Billy explained.

'You're right, there is a tall wall surrounding the sanctuary and at every huge gate of it, there is an army of soldiers guarding it. Guarding mrunnas from men and men from mrunnas' Jimmy explained.

'Once the battle is complete and if mrunnas have won, how are you planning to get them inside the sanctuary?' Billy asked.

'The same way I would have led them out of the sanctuary. By using the same young I have captured and making them follow me back to their rightful habitat,' I explained.

'You need to tell the king about your plan and he will help you put your plan into action, but before you have won the arena season, no one will think of you as worthy of anything,' Billy said.

'He is right, mate. You've gotta prove yourself in the arena in front of everybody and the king first,' Jimmy said.

With that, the pain in the wounds in my back returned. Jimmy helped me by applying the doctor's healing ointment on my back, and after that, I took a long nap.

The Arena Season Arrives

The season was here finally and I was getting dressed for the arena. As my managers, it was the twin brothers' responsibility to get some paperwork signed at the arena so they had left an hour ago and given me the key to lock the cottage behind on my way to the arena.

When I reached the same double door of the arena when I had been there upon enrolling my name with the clerk, I saw that it was wide open and I heard the faint roar of a cheering crowd of thousands of spectators. It reminded me of the same arena I had been in my dream back in the prison at the events of the yellow lotus. I survived there, barely, would I do the same here? I thought.

The twin brothers then showed up in the doorway. Jimmy grabbed my elbow and led me inside, and after fancying about it for days in my mind, I entered the mighty arena for the first time.

He led me to a special section of seats for spectating that was reserved for the contestants of the season. My seat was way back. But the arrangement of the seats was in such a way that the seats rose a bit as you went back.

Some of the seats in the contestant's section were already filled, but as I waited there the remaining seats gradually became occupied. The chatter among the friendly contestants continued until half an hour had passed. Then, half a dozen women and men entered the down in the arena. I didn't know what they were about. They surely hadn't dressed as warriors. Then suddenly drumming men entered the arena and men and women began dancing. It must be some kind of ceremony before the season began, I thought.

The king himself then entered the arena once the dance had finished. He was followed by two of the heavily armoured guards. At the king's entrance applause could be heard all around the arena. Upon the king's gesture, two of the men entered the arena and walked to stand in front of the king. The king then pulled his sword from the sheath at his hip and rested the tip of it on each of the shoulders of both men. After that, the king, his two guards and the drumming and dancing men and women left the arena and a musical instrument honked loudly, fit to wake the dead. Then from somewhere dozens of drums began to sound and the reaming two warrior-like dressed men shook each other's hand and took a position on a line opposite each other. The distance between the two lines couldn't have been more than ten paces long.

Once the king had reached his booth of spectating, the very first battle of the season began. Both men wielded a heavy long swords and both of them began swinging their swords at each other.

The contest lasted for fifteen minutes before the loser was murdered by being impaled by the sword in his throat by his opponent, and instantly I was reminded that it was no longer a contest but a bloodsport. People lost their lives here. It was no ordinary arena but a ring of death. God knows how many lives would have been taken away before the season finally ended, I thought.

Followed by the death of the loser, the victorious man bowed to his dead opponent and left the arena ring. Moments later, a couple of men brought out a wooden plank and carried the dead man out of the ring on it.

Five minutes later, two other contestants entered the ring and after the handshake of respect began battling each other. One was wielding a pike and the other a double-edged axe. Like the previous, this battle was over in under fifteen minutes and another the one with the pike lost and died. There came the men with plank and the dead body was carried out of the ring.

For the next three hours, the contestants in the contestant's section began to leave their seats and entered the arena to kill or get killed. It was a bloodbath for an hour. When it was over, my turn hadn't come to enter the ring. I even had doubts if I had been enrolled in the arena season or not in the first place. But then, there were hundreds of contestants still sitting in the contestant's section who hadn't been summoned to fight and were awaiting their turn.

We spent the rest of the day fishing at the lake and before sunset we had reached the safety of the cottage. The whole night was passed hiding beneath a blanket, trying to get some sleep in the cacophony of the terrifying roars made by raks all night long.

As soon as the morning came, taking out fresh pair of clothes, we headed for the lake. There, after taking the bath in the lake and putting on fresh clothes and washing up the dirty ones, we returned to the cottage. After setting things proper in the cottage we wasted no time heading to the arena.

Once again I was seated in the contestant's section and looked down at the ring. Over half an hour, seats began to fill up with spectators and other contestants. Today was the second day of the season and there was no ceremony. Only there were battles. The king was in his booth up high guarded by his soldiers.

Eardrum-shattering sound of conches resonated across the whole arena and two of the contestants entered the ring. Both stood at their lines facing them. Then I saw something that just almost made me jump in my seat with surprise. One of the contestants was female and it was no other than Athena!

The crowd then suddenly began to chant a name ....Lilith...Lilith... I was confused at that. Who was Lilith? She certainly wasn't in the ring.

At a gesture from the king, the drummers started banging their drums and the battle began. Athena and her opponent, who was a bearded, muscular man, left their lines and began circling. The heat was rising between the two of them and the crowd did everything it could to raise the roof with excitement. These two must be champions because the crowd was going crazy with shouts, roaring and clapping. For this particular match, the whole arena had become alive. The king himself was at his feet, spectating the match with excitement.

Athena threw a throwing knife, but it was deflected by the man with his long and heavy-looking sword. He then charged toward Athena and began to swing his sword at her. I had my fingers crossed for Athena. I certainly didn't want anyone to die, but I hope it wouldn't be Athena who would lose the match.

Athena brought out a sword of herself and began blocking the blows. Two of them continued to battle each other with swords until Athena kicked the man in the gut and the man sort of bowed grabbing his belly. Athena took the opening and struck a powerful round kick to his head. The man got knocked cold. Afterwards, Athena slit his throat with her sword. It was brutal to watch the kill. Athena had won and the whole arena once again came to life with roars and cheers. There was the chanting of the name by the arena crowd...Lilith...Lilith...Lilith...

The whole match lasted for fifteen minutes. Two men brought out a wooden stretcher and carried the dead body of the loser out of the ring. Immediately, two men in the contestant's section disappeared, to appear in the ring the next minutes. The king gave a gesture, drums began and so did the battle.

It had been for four hours the battles continued. Once it was over it was late afternoon already. There had been breaks in between fights and we had used them to eat food that was served for free to the contestants and their agents.

With the day's battle session over we were on our way to the cottage now. 'Did you see the first fight Lilith won? It was amazing,' Jimmy said while walking.

'Yeah, brother. Lilith is an example of what women can do,' Billy said.

'Lilith?' I asked in confusion. 'You mean, Athena?'

'Who's Athena?' Billy asked.

Then an explanation dawned on me. Here, it was not the same realm. Everyone was bounded to be here but with a different identity. Even I could stumble upon myself bearing a different name. 'So, it was not Athena but Lilith,' I thought out a bit loudly.

'What are you saying, bruh?' Jimmy asked.

'It is nothing, I was just...Yeah, Lilith did well. She sure is a force to be reckoned with,' I said.

'Damn right, you are,' Jimmy said.

'By the way, we checked the brackets in the arena. Tomorrow you will be entering the ring in the third battle. It will be a man called Jack. He's an archer,' Billy said.

'So, you'd better prepare yourself for tomorrow, mate. You could practise with us during the whole night. We have a few sticks and dummy shields at the cottage. You could practice with them,' Jimmy said.

'Thanks, guys. Sure I would practice, but I'll be relying on my magic in the arena battle and it would be dangerous to practice with them in the cottage,' I said.

At that Jimmy nodded. 'In that case, we will see you using your magic in the arena ring then.'

CHAPTER FIVE

The Bloody War Of The Beasts

The next day came and I was in the lobby reserved for combatants. There were five other men seated inside the lobby. Two of them exited the door and entered the arena. I heard the loud resonance of the conches and beating of drums, suggesting that the first battle had begun. I sat there in the lobby for fifteen minutes before I saw a dead man being carried on a wooden stretcher inside a lobby and placed into one of the lined empty caskets in a corner. The winner entered the lobby boasting of his victory and left from the other door.

Another two men entered the arena after ten minutes and there was a roar of a cheering crowd, telling that the match was going to be interesting. Conches resonated and drums began which must have followed the battle.

The battle was over as soon as it had started and the lobby door was flung open by two men carrying a dead combatant on a stretcher who filled the next coffin in the corner. Soon after that the twin brothers entered the lobby from the back door and walked to stand in front of me.

'You're next brother. Here is the sword you asked for,' Jimmy said while handing me a double-edged light sword.

'Let your opponent go first,' Billy said as a short man of my height exited the lobby via the front door and entered the arena ring. We waited for two minutes before Jimmy patted lightly on my shoulder, suggesting that it was a go time for me.

The twin brothers followed me to the door and then I entered the ring alone but with my sword resting in a scabbard provided free by the arena management. The bright light of the afternoon blinded me as I entered from the dark lobby to the sunlit arena ring.

When my eyes had adjusted I saw that the whole ring was bigger than it had looked from the spectator's stand. The land was dry with patches of dust here and there. Such minor details were not possible from the spectating seats. I saw that my opponent had already taken a position at his line and was waiting for me to take one.

I nervously strode to my mark of the line while looking down. The crowd was on its feet and cheering the name Lucas....Lucas...Lucas which must be my opponent's name. I saw the king staring down at both of us contestants and he gave a gesture by clapping both hands. At that, couples of conches resonated and drums began to beat. I touched my amulet which was tied with a strong chain around my neck.

The man left his line and darted toward me while shouting as if I were his sworn enemy and he needed to put his blades through me. A blade in each hand of his looked mighty sharp, fit to cut me with buttery smoothness. I'd better be careful or I would be the one to fill the next coffin in the corner of the lobby.

When my opponent was no farther than a few paces away, I unfurled my magical wings of angels and leapt high above his head. At that move, the audience gasped with surprise. I landed immediately behind my opponent and thrust my sword into the right thigh of the man, taking out his ability to run. While dropping both swords on the ground and clutching his would with both hands, the man dropped to both knees.

I was surely victorious and I didn't want to prove that by killing the man, so I dropped my blade and at that the drums and crowd went silent. I was booed by all of the thousands of spectators. Ignoring them, I turned to exit the ring, but soldiers entered the ring suddenly and surrounded me.

One of them spoke while reading from a paper, 'You've disrespected the arena by not abiding by its rules. Here, it is the contract you signed and it says you'll accept any punishment deemed worthy for such infringement. So, to the dungeon, you will go.'

*

I sat in the dimly lit room behind the iron bars. This is the second time I had been put into a dungeon. The first time Maggie had hired a thief to lead me out of the dungeon. I didn't know how I was going to get out. No sooner had that thought entered my mind than there were earthquakes, shaking the ground tremendously. A minute later there were soldiers in the corridor freeing other prisoners. One of the soldiers came to free me.

'All of the mrunnas have climbed out of the sanctuary walls and are waging war with raks. It's a bloody battle up there,' the soldier said while he tried to unlock the cell's door. 'You're lucky that we are escorting all prisoners to the ground. The lower floors might collapse by the tremors being created by the battle between mrunnas and raks.'

'What caused them to go at each other?' I asked.

'Reports from the posted men at the sanctuary tell that a couple of raks flew past the sanctuary walls and killed one of the baby mrunnas. Those giant white apes didn't take that lightly and chased the raks all the way here. There are probably dozens of mrunnas up there on the ground battling a legion of raks. Seems like, at the end of the battle, one of the sides would perish completely. Either it is the end of mrunnas or raks, only the time will tell.'

With a grating sound, the cell's door opened and I stepped over the threshold. 'Follow me. And don't make an attempt of breaking free,' the soldier said and led me to the stone steps and we climbed to the ground level.

I was led out of the arena building and into the open. I was being escorted out of the arena and to the nearest fortress of the king. I could see the bloody mess on the ground everywhere. There were dead bodies of mrunnas and raks everywhere. The air was filled with raks attacking mrunnas and everything that moved on the ground. I saw one mrunna jump in the air and take down a giant rak. I saw a couple of raks lifting a heavy mrunna off the ground and taking it in the air before ripping it into pieces.

As I was being escorted to a cart that would take us to a nearby fortress, my captor was lifted by a swooping rak and torn into pieces. A couple more swooped down and lifted the cart high in the sky and threw it down on the ground. The cart was smashed like a little child's toy. With my captor killed, I was free to flee. Not knowing where to go, I ran to the twin brothers' cottage. I ran from building to building, hiding from raks' and mrunnas' sights, When suddenly, the ground shook like hell is about to go loose and I saw a very gigantic rak sitting where it had used to be the arena. And for the arena, there was no sign of it because the rak was so giant that the arena was crushed to rubble under its weight. It was as big as the arena itself and when it had landed on the ground, that must have sent tremors to the ground that I had felt.

When I thought mrunnas were done for against that giant mother rak, a thunderous roar sounded from the east. Moments later a white ape, an adult mrunna probably, of the size to match the mother rak showed up. It beat its chest loudly a couple of times before sprinting on all fours towards the mother rak.

I kept watching for the first two minutes as the two titans clashed under the moonlight sky. After two minutes, I made my way hastily but carefully towards the cottage. When I reached at last while staying hidden from the sights of normal raks and mrunnas, I banged the door loudly three times in the cacophony of the ongoing battle, hoping the twin brothers had returned safely to the cottage. To my relief, the door was answered and I saw Jimmy gesturing for me to get in quickly. I just did that, and behind me, the door was quickly closed and locked up. Inside, Billy was filling kerosene into one of the lanterns and was happy to see me.

'Think we'll be safe in here?' I asked.

'There is nowhere else to go,' Billy said.

'I hope, this cottage of ours provides us protection from the battle,' I said.

'Not if one of those two titan beasts stepped on it,' Jimmy said.

'I saw them battling at the arena, which is quite far from here. I hope they don't come here fighting,' I said.

With that, we just sat in our beds and stared at the wall and ceiling, hearing the noise of the battle between mrunnas and raks. By the morning one side would lose and perish, and I hoped it to be of raks. Because, once the battle was over, I knew that mrunnas would return to their sanctuary peacefully, but the terror of raks would continue if they survived the war.

Actually, it was my plan to pit two of the kinds at each other, but I didn't know that the results would be so devastating.

*

When the sun came, the tranquillity returned, suggesting the end of the war. We soon found good news, that was, mrunnas were victorious and the people of the village no longer needed to fear raks because they were no more. In one night the ages-long terror had perished, thanks to mrunnas. I could now get the two hearts of mrunnas and present them to the soul collector. According to the twin brothers, its floating kingdom was in the sky. It would have been impossible in my realm to have a soul collector and floating kingdom nonsense. But it was not my realm and anything could go here.

I found two dead mrunnas nearby the cottage and had to do the gruesome work of cutting out the hearts from their chests. It was a nasty piece of work but someone had to do it. I placed them in a canvas bag I got from the twin brothers and after tying it at my back I said my farewell to the twin brothers.

'Thanks, guys for all the help and the hospitality,' I said, 'I will never forget you two. And I'm sorry that I couldn't get you the prize money of the arena.'

'Nah. I am happy that the ring of murder is destroyed at last. There would be no more competition for killing people over mrunna's heart,' Jimmy said.

'They could still rebuild the arena,' Billy said.

'But it would be much time before that happens,' Jimmy said.

'Yeah, that's right. And with raks gone, once again people of the village could resume their normal lives at night,' Billy said.

With the canvas bag behind my back, I unfurled my magical wings and after nodding my gratitude at the twin brothers I took flight and made my way in the sky to the floating kingdom of the soul collector 'Dar'.

CHAPTER SIX

The Floating Kingdom

I had flown for six hours straight in the sky towards the direction provided by the twin brothers before I started to see a black speck in the sky. As I moved closer to it, the speck started to grow bigger. Gradually it took shape and I started to see a bedrock with a few buildings visible from my point of view. As I gained altitude and levelled to the bedrock, I saw that there was a whole city on it.

I looked down and saw that a part of the traditional world beneath was visible to my eyes. I thought of how much time it would take for a piece of rock to land beneath from up here. Probably much time.

A mighty tall wall was built upon the rim of the bedrock. The wall was as tall as ten meters and I had to gain extra altitude to get past those walls and gain entrance into the city. I landed on a small bridge over a canal. I was astonished by the nature it had as same as that of the land of mine way beneath. I was wondering how this whole kingdom floated high up in the air.

Then I saw a bunch of people around me. They were all naked. In resemblance, they looked just like simple men of my land except their bodies were way thinner and their heads were bigger. They looked to be so much at peace that only dead people could compete with them at being calm.

A naked young woman passed by me on the bridge and my mind just took an understanding of something which felt like someone had just greeted and welcomed me to this kingdom. I called the naked lady to stop. She obeyed and turned with a happy expression; In fact, everyone around me had expressions of being happy and it was getting very weird.

'Miss, why you and other people here are not wearing clothes?' I asked.

She just smiled and spoke with a very mild and weak voice, 'We, here, do not need such a thing. We have connected to parmatma and it has provided us with the energy to shield our bodies against cold, heat and other natural phenomena. And socially talking, our minds have simply lifted up from petty things such as seeing or getting seen naked and feeling weird about it.'

I shot more questions that were swirling in my mind. 'How come you guys have different bodies than mine?'

'We, here, consume different food than yours and use different organs than yours to digest it,' she said.

'What are you talking about? Which type of food?' I asked.

'Sun's and moon's energy is what we consume via our bodies' various receptors. It gives us different kinds of energy. The energy that we borrow from parmatma and give it back,' she said.

'Who is this parmatma that you speak of?' I asked getting confused by the minute.

'Parmatma is the creator of everything. It is a tiny dot from which everything living and non-living spawned. We should always be grateful to Parmatma. Everything is a part of parmatma's immense body. You are a part of parmatma, I'm a part of parmatma, that small piece of rock over there is a part of parmatma,' she explained.

'Is parmatma a god?' I asked scratching my head stupidly.

'No. God is a god and parmatma is parmatma. The creatures who get connected with the divine energy of parmatma become gods. Just like us people here in this kingdom called Sarg. Centuries ago we enlighted ourselves with the blessing from parmatma.

'You see, we were no different than you back then. Cutting trees, building shelters, fighting over wealth, poisoned with envy, anger and lust, destroying ourselves and the world and hurting parmatma in the process. But ever since a man called John taught us all the way to get connected with parmatma and achieve the ultimate enlightenment, our world has changed upside down, for good. He first taught us to abandon the practice of inferior food consumption ways and showed us the practice of superior food consumption ways. It was hard at first but when we finally learned it, it was the beginning of the end of the hell we were used to live in.

'We were taught other many things like being one with nature and developing various skills such as telepathy and telekinesis,' she explained.

'Tele....what?' I asked, hearing the term for the first time.

'Telepathy and telekinesis. The ability to communicate without speaking and the ability to move things with your mind,' she explained. 'Then we just continued to develop more skills and it would be the night if I started to speak out all the skills we know here in Sarg.'

'How come this kingdom became floating?' I asked finally.

'It's the combined mind and spiritual energy of us all people here on Sarg to keep this kingdom afloat,' she said smiling. 'By the way, what brings you here, young master?'

'I'm here to see Dar, the soul collector,' I replied honestly.

'Let me guess. You want your loved ones to be alive once again?'

'Yes,' I nodded.

'Have you brought the hearts of mrunnas?' she asked.

'It's here in my bag,' I turned to show the bag tied to my back.

'Very well,' she said and she forged a bubble of energy around us two and we began floating towards the north of the kingdom.

*

For twenty minutes the bubble floated and during that time I saw the whole of the kingdom from a bird-eye view. There were more naked people about beneath and their simpler homes were visible all across the forested kingdom. There were rivers, canals, waterfalls and miniature mountains. This floating kingdom had the best scenery I had ever witnessed.

'We are still trying to forge a shelter of energy so that we can abandon our traditional ways of having a shelter to protect us from rain, heat and cold. We are still working on that,' she explained. And with that, we arrived at a huge fortress wall. The naked lady left me at the giant gates of the fortress wall and left by floating away in the bubble without saying anything but smile.

I pushed the gate and it opened smoothly. Inside there was a fine garden with exquisite-looking topiaries of animals. Among the various shapes of animals made of shrubs, I found a topiary of a mrunna. I walked to the fountain that lay in the middle and observed more of the surrounding. The stone fortress lay fifteen paces away.

Then suddenly, the fortress door opened and two naked men came out.

'Greetings, human. Please state your business,' one of the naked men said.

'I'm here to see Dar, the soul collector, to exchange two souls with mrunna hearts,' I said.

'Follow us,' the other naked man said and he led me into the fortress.

Once I entered the fortress I got a feeling of happiness about getting to see Mr Smith and Athena soon. In the hall, I saw two stairs leading up and I was led from the left one. When I had been escorted into a chamber I was left alone. The chamber door was closed and I saw a shape forming before my eyes. A moment later I was seeing a bald naked man floating before me. He was sitting in the air crosslegged and his hand formed a namaste gesture.

'Greetings, young Frank. I'm Dar, the soul collector and I know why you're here,' Dar spoke.

I said nothing but returned the gesture of namaste and bowed my hands before placing the bag on the floor.

'I shall give you the soul of your friends Randolph and Athena in exchange for these divine organs,' Dar spoke. 'Have you brought a vessel to carry these souls I'm about to give you?'

I didn't have to speak anything because he had just read my mind. 'Yes, your majesty,' I said for the first time before him and showed him the earthen jar Eliza had given to me.

'Good, here it is then,' Dar said and with a series of gestures of his hands the jar I was holding became heavy, suggesting that the souls had been transferred to it.

'You may leave now, young Frank and you may take your empty bag with you,' Dar said and he vanished in the thin air.

What empty bag, I thought to myself. Then it occurred to me to check the canvas bag which held mrunnas' hearts. I found it to be empty.

The chamber door opened and the two naked men returned and escorted me out of the fortress. Once out of the fortress wall, the same naked lady that had brought me here was waiting outside.

'Did you acquire what you were looking for from Dar?' she asked.

I nodded. She had helped me and I hadn't even asked her name, I thought.

'It's Maya, young Frank,' she said after she had read my mind. She seemed to know everything in my mind as I simply made any thoughts. 'Let's get back to the former spot we just met at,' so saying she formed a bubble around us and we began floating away from the fortress.

'Dar is the one who taught us the way of becoming one with the parmatma. He is the reason that Sarg exists,' Maya said.

'But you said John taught you all about divine ways of living,' I asked.

'He is John but he goes by the name Dar now. Ever since parmatma tasked him with the work of reincarnation of souls, he has been very busy. He locks up in his private chamber the whole day and night. If he is not meditating then he is asleep. He says sleeping is a divine tool of gods that must be practised,' Maya said.

'We have many sayings and one of them is "You snooze, you lose"' I said smiling.

'How can you lose while practising the divine tool of parmatma?' Maya said.

'I mean if everybody went to sleeping all day, who would do the work?' I asked.

'What work?' Maya asked.

'You know, lumbering, farming, doing guard duty, running post wagons and so on...?' I said.

'Your people think that without these works they can't survive? Well, that's wrong. You're not supposed to do such petty tasks for your own survival. Parmatma has created ways to make us survive without doing a thing. All we have to do is perform the tasks we are entitled to do in return,' Maya explained.

'And what are those tasks?' I asked.

'To protect the world and the universe with your vast spiritual energy. Take out the sufferings of other inferior beings and keep the world a happy place to live in,' Maya explained. 'You see for your own survival, parmatma has made arrangements.'

I nodded thoughtfully, and then the rest of the journey was silent.

*

We arrived back at the canal bridge and I was wondering why Maya had brought us back here. But then she said, 'It will be here in a moment.'

'Who will be here?' I asked.

'Your friend the divine tigress,' Maya said.

No sooner had she said that than a thump sounded from behind me and I turned to see the familiar figure. It was the divine tigress. Its one eye had been gouged out by Sirius' pet dragon in a battle over the mountain of the divine tigress.

'She had come to see you, young Frank,' Maya said. 'She lives here in Sarg now and she wants to say goodbye to you before you leave. That's why I brought you here.'

'But I saw her in my realm. How could she exists here?' I asked.

'She has an ability to enter into different realms, young Frank. Now go on, she's been waiting for you ever since she found out you were here,' Maya said.

I walked to the tigress and patted her down. She gave a mild growl from her throat. After a moment she bowed down and flew away. Then there was a clap of thunder. I looked about in the sky and found no clouds that may have given that thunder. The thunderous sound came again.

'This doesn't feel right. The attack should have been a week from now foreseen by Dar,' Maya said looking into the sky.

'What attack, Maya? What are you talking about?' I asked.

'Dar had been seeing images in his mind of a foreign being coming in their vessels to attack this world. Dar somehow figured out that they would attack this floating kingdom first and move their attacks to the world below. Those swords, arrows and pikes of men won't stand a chance against destructive weapons of theirs,' Maya explained and there came another clap of thunder.

'What are you gonna do?' I asked.

'We would raise an energy shield surrounding the floating kingdom Sarg. It will block any of the weapons from shooting destructive lights at us. By now, as Dar instructed, all of the people on Sarg would have connected their energies to that of Dar and Dar would have been preparing to forge a shield in a minute or two. Forgive me but I've to concentrate to connect to the energy of dar and contribute my powers to the shield,' Maya said and sat down and went into a trance.

I stood there listening to more thunderclaps. Five minutes later there was a blueish transparent glass covering Sarg.

Another ten minutes later Maya woke up from the trance and stood up. 'I've done my bit and the shield is now alive,' Maya said. No sooner she had said that than a dozen of huge vessels emerged from the sky. Their emergence was so sudden that they could have been popped in from the thin air.

'Here they come,' Maya warned.

The vessels travelled near the floating kingdom and once near Sarg, they attacked it with their destructive purple lights. The shield soaked most of the impact but some of it managed to enter through the shield and impacted the bedrock, sending tremors across the kingdom.

'Stand back, young Frank, I shall attack them now with my own destructive light,' So Maya said and began sending light beams at the flying vessels. The beam passed through the shield smoothly and hit a vessel, giving a small explosion on impact. Maya continued to attack with her deadly light beams as the vessels tried hard to breach the protective shield of Sarg.

Half an hour passed and the shield was intact, so vessels stopped their bombardment. The foreign beings were now leaving their ships and flying with fiery machines attached to their backs. They managed to fly through the shield and landed on Sarg. No sooner they had landed than there was a bloodbath. They began shooting projectiles from the machines they held in their hands and started killing people of Sarg with them. The beings looked just like normal men but with the colour of their skin blue. The people of Sarg fought back with the energy attacks and took down some of the blue people.

I wanted to help defend the people of Sarg and fight the blue people so I activated my aura of shiv and unfurled my magical wings and took flight. With the help of the Bow of Rama I took out dozens of blue people but it more were pouring in by the minute from the ship, So I retreated back to where Maya was fighting.

'Are you seeing that big vessel?' Maya asked while throwing energy bolts at the army of blue people.

'Yes,' I screamed over the cacophony of war.

'That's the mother vessel. Powerful enough to destroy everything in its path,' Maya shouted.

'Yeah? How does that help us?' I asked shouting.

'If we get to the mother vessels and control it, we can use it to destroy all of the other vessels around it and that would stop the blue people from pouring in in Sarg,' She shouted.

'But how we will control it? I wouldn't know how they work,' I shouted.

'I do. Just use your wings to take me swiftly to the mother vessel and I will handle the rest,' She shouted.

I did as she had said and I gave her the piggy ride to the ship. I saw a door from which blue people were exiting the gigantic mother vessel. We killed some and entered through the red-shielded energy door. As soon as we entered the vessel we were attacked. Thanks to the aura of the shiv and the protective bubble formed by Maya around us, the light beams were deflected off its surface and we remained unharmed. Maya and I then began an attack of ours and took out as many blue people as possible before fighting our way to the control chamber.

Once in the control chamber, we took out the remaining force there and took control of the mother vessel. There were hundreds of buttons, levers and blinking lights in the control chamber. I had no idea how what to do, but Maya did. She hurried back and forth flipping levers, and switches, and pushing various buttons. From the weird-looking white boxes with glasses, I saw everything around me that happened. Maya destroyed all of the flying vessels and then pressed a big red button before telling me to hurry out of the mother vessel. From somewhere in the vessel, a woman began counting down numbers from sixty.

We exited from the same red energy door we had entered and no sooner we had exited and flown away a bit, explosion after explosion began destroying the vessel. It was daytime but still, the sky went bright with the light of the explosions. The vessel then lost its altitude and crashed on the ground below, throwing debris and dust around on impact.

Now all that remained was taking out the infantry force on Sarg. It took us half an hour to send all the blue people to hell, but in the process, many of our men and women had perished fighting back. The divine tigress had also helped to defend Sarg.

Once it was over, I asked Maya about who were these blue people and why they wanted to attack. She replied, 'They were men and women just like you and me but climbed up on the wrong wagon of evolution. You see, they chose to cut trees rather than learn from them, they chose to kill animals and other lives rather than help them. They chose to stick with the satanic food and satanic tongue that forced them to fight against each other over the centuries. When the resources in their world for their satanic way of life were depleted they were forced to conquer another world for fresh new supplies. Parmatma knows how many worlds they have conquered and destroyed before they came over here for this.

'You need to spread the message to your people not to turn into one of those blue people but adopt the ways of the divine and make Sarg everywhere,' Maya said.

*

I was passing through a portal to my home realm and when I stood once again outside the shop of Eliza I had a feeling of happiness at what I had achieved. Purging a village off the terror of nocturnal creatures and defeating foreign people from conquering a world. And as if it was not enough, I would soon be awakening Randolph and Athena from their eternal slumber.

To be continued...

Other books available from the author
    Something Strange Over The Yellow Lotus
    Macabre Expedition
    At The Mountain Of The Divine Tigress
    Steven Johnson And The Mission 1
    Steven Johnson And The Mission 2
    I, The Rebel
    The Path Of A Rebel